By Jennifer Waters Howells

Illustrated by Kelsey Dzintars
Edited by Joseph O'Connor

In the deepest blue sea, off the shore of a beautiful island, lived a mermaid named Marie.

Every day Marie dreamed of
being a ballerina, but she was
born in the sea and had fins
instead of feet.

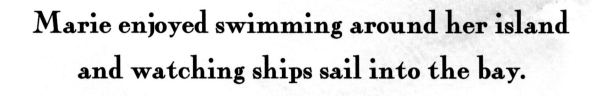

Marie enjoyed swimming around her island
and watching ships sail into the bay.

As the ships sailed closer Marie could see beautiful
ballerinas performing on the deck for the guests. She would
curl up alongside her favorite rock and watch for hours,
imagining herself in their shoes.

As much as Marie enjoyed watching the mesmerizing dancers, watching also made her very sad and she would cry. She wondered, "Why can't I be a ballerina? Why was I born in the sea?"

One day on her way home from her favorite rock, Marie
happened to swim through some pretty, pink, soft weeds.
"Seaweed," she thought, "how interesting." But these
plants are usually brown or green, not pink.

Looking closer, Marie was astonished to find ribbons, not seaweed. At the end of the ribbons, she found a pair of beautiful ballerina shoes.

"I wonder how these beautiful shoes ended up at the bottom the sea," thought Marie.

She knew she could not wear them since she had fins instead of feet, but decided to take them home anyway.

Marie happily swam home with her new shoes, but by this time it was getting late.

When she arrived, her mother told her it was bedtime. Marie quietly tucked the shoes under her pillow, in hopes of having sweet ballerina dreams.

Her mom came in and said, "Good night Marie. Lights out, please." Marie said good night to her mom and decided to take one more look at her new, pink, beautiful ballerina shoes.

"I have an idea," Marie whispered to herself. "I think I'll try these on my fins, just to see what they look like."

As Marie slipped the shoes on her fins, she started twirling up and out of her bed through the water and right out of the sea!

She had long legs and pointed feet, just like the ballerinas she had seen. Marie floated up and up into the sky and landed gracefully on the deck of the ship where the ballerinas perform.

"Is this a dream? Are these magical ballerina shoes?"
thought Marie. She was spinning and leaping across
the stage as all the ship guests applauded. She was
performing with the same ballerinas she had watched
from her favorite rock.

The ballerinas ran offstage after the performance. Marie tried to follow them but as she ran she was again floating in the sky above the ship like a delicate, dancing butterfly.

With all the dancing, Marie was beginning to get sleepy. It was getting late and she worried that her mom might come into her room to check on her. She wasn't sure what to do. She decided to take off her beautiful, magical ballerina shoes.

Marie untied the ribbons on her beautiful ballerina shoes. Her fins reappeared and she dove into the water and swam home.

She quickly went to bed and put her shoes under her pillow once again, in hopes of having sweet ballerina dreams.

Marie was so
tired she fell
into a deep sleep.

Buzzzzzzzz...went Marie's alarm. It was time for her to wake up.

The first thing Marie did as she awoke was check under her pillow for her beautiful, magical ballerina shoes.

They were not there. Marie decided to look under her bed to see if they had slipped from beneath her pillow in the middle of the night. She still could not find her shoes.

What Marie found
was that she had feet and
long legs, just like in
her dream.

Where were her fins?
How would she swim
to her favorite rock to
watch the ballerinas?

As Marie was feeling sad and confused,
her mother came into her room and said,
"Marie, it's time for ballet," and handed
her a bag filled with ballerina shoes,
tights, a leotard, and even a tutu!

Marie awoke to find that she wasn't a Mermaid after all. She had been a ballerina all along!

Published by Dancing Waters Press, LLC
PO Box 161888
Big Sky, Montana 59716

Paperback ISBN: 978-0-9988628-1-1

Printed in the United States of America

www.mariesdream.com • www.dancingwaterspress.com

Made in the USA
Middletown, DE
07 May 2017